P9-EEP-295

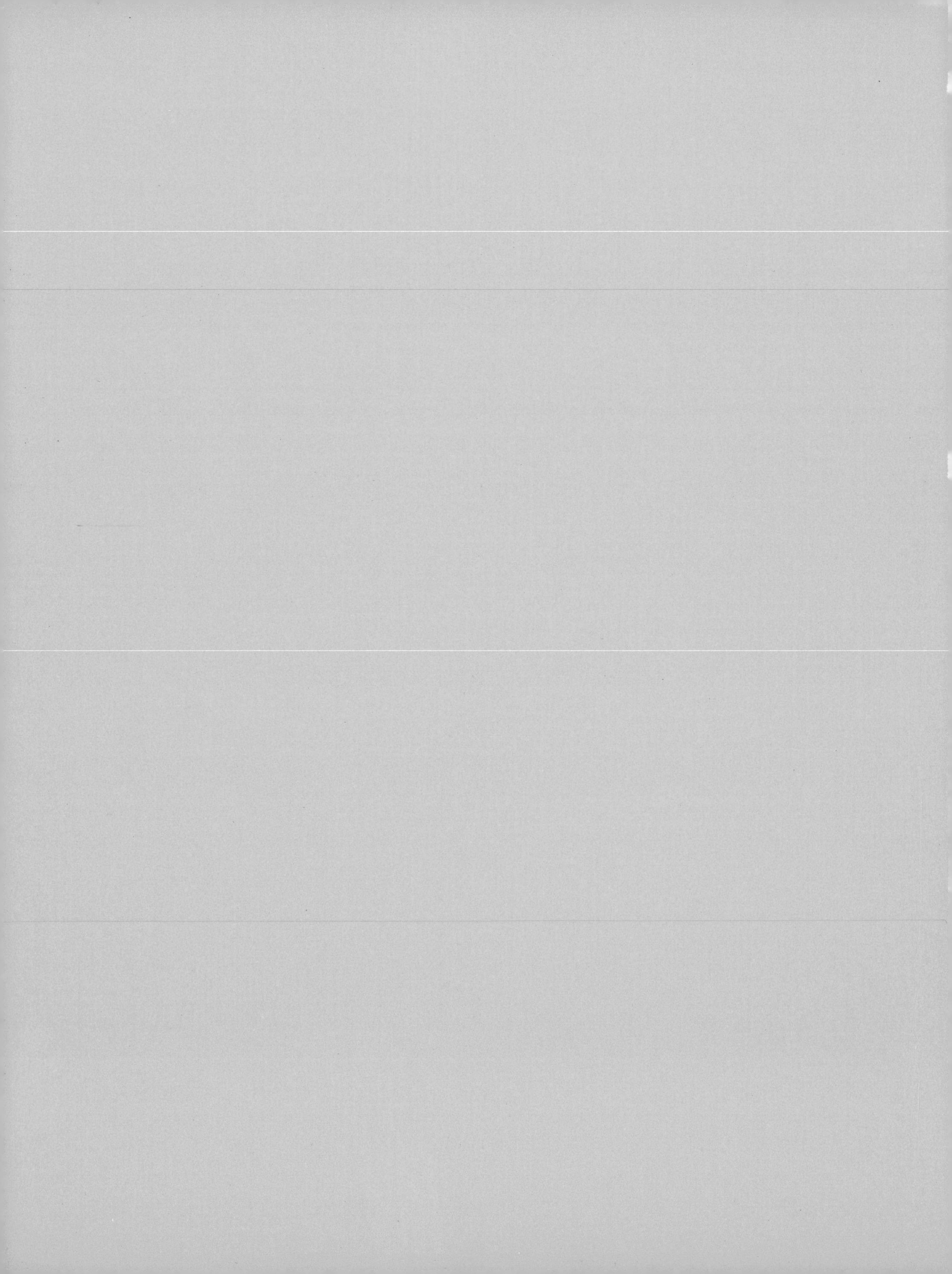

HONEY PAW
and LIGHTFOOT

by JONATHAN LONDON

Illustrated by JON VAN ZYLE

In the bushy willow bottomland
Honey Paw ambled,
stopped, sniffed.

On a rock spine, against sky,
stood Old Man of the Mountains.
Honey Paw watched as Old Man
scrambled down the rock slide.
The closer he came
the bigger he looked.

It was June, the mating moon of grizzlies,
and that night, under stars,
the two great bears became a pair.
Over the next days,
they browsed together,
tossed their great heads,
and chased each other.

But one morning Honey Paw
rambled on, hungry for berries,
and Old Man went his own way
up in the mountains.

All summer, Honey Paw read the wind and the mysteries of the rivers, seeking food. And in the fall she ate to get fat for winter.

Days grew short, nights grew long.

Honey Paw sensed the snows rolling in.

She dug a den on a slope
away from the wind.
Made a bed of bear grass,
moss, and boughs of young fir.
Finished, just in time.
For soon the big snows came.

Then Honey Paw snuggled warm in her soft bed,
and snored in a sleep so deep—
her heartbeat so slow—
you might think she'd sleep forever.

Moons passed. Drifts piled.

Finally, in the heart of winter
Lightfoot was born.
Helpless, almost hairless, blind,
no bigger than a hamster.
He nursed in the deep dark
warmth of his mother's den.

Come spring, two moons later,
Honey Paw and Lightfoot awoke.
Lightfoot bumbled out,
blinking in the sunshine,
a furry ball of hunger.

He followed
as his mother hunted and grazed
and dug for roots,
showing her cub good foods to eat.

If Lightfoot strayed, Honey Paw swatted him back into line. But not all was the business of finding food; mother and cub liked to play.

Swoosh! Honey Paw and Lightfoot
plunged down the slopes
skidding to a stop in a shower of slush.
Again and again—*swoosh!*—sliding on belly,
back, and rump, rolling head over tail.

All through spring,
Honey Paw and Lightfoot
loped and ambled, eating
bear grass, bear flowers, bear clover,
and—if they were lucky—honey.
Every two or three hours
Lightfoot stopped
to nurse. He nuzzled his mother
and drank: warm rich milk.

After eating, they would sleep the hot hours
on a day bed dug in the soft earth.

The one day, toward the end of spring,
a huge grizzly, Big Hairy One,
lumbered down over deadfall,
the muscles of his great flanks rippling.

With a sudden roar, Big Hairy One came galloping
after Lightfoot, fast as a racehorse.
Lightfoot scrambled away.
He could feel Hairy One's breath.
Honey Paw lunged between them.
Lightfoot slid beneath her legs,
tumbled into the river
and was swept away.

The last Lightfoot heard
as he wailed and rolled down the current
was his mother's roar rumbling off the cliffs.

Lightfoot tumbled and choked in the white water.

Hooked a snag.

Climbed up. And waited,

shivering in the spray.

As the dark dropped, and the moon rose,

Lightfoot yowled, but did not let go.

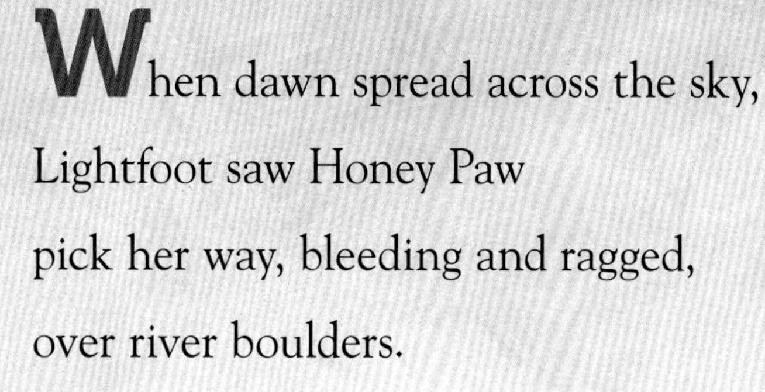

When dawn spread across the sky,
Lightfoot saw Honey Paw
pick her way, bleeding and ragged,
over river boulders.

At last, Honey Paw reached up,
above the roar of the waterfall,
snatched her cub, and held him tight.
Lightfoot was safe!

Honey Paw couldn't play with Lightfoot until her wounds had healed.

A moon passed.
And another moon.
Then one day, Honey Paw
bent a willow bush over for him,
and when Lightfoot jumped on,
Honey Paw let the bush spring up . . .

and Lightfoot flipped into the river. *Splash!*

Through another year
of moons and seasons Lightfoot grew,
learning from Honey Paw
where to feast on the juiciest roots
and berries, dig the best den,
and find the best places to play.
Soon Lightfoot would be ready
to go off on his own.

A Note from the Author

Honey Paw, Lightfoot, Old Man of the Mountains, Big Hairy One. For Native Americans, and native people all across Eurasia, to speak the name "bear" was to evoke its power. Instead, out of respect for the bears, they were given nicknames. Grandfather of the Hill, Grandmother, Strong One, the One Who Owns the Den. These and other nicknames were used by the Finns, Tungus, Lapps, and Blackfoot Indians, among other tribal peoples across the Northern Hemisphere.

The bears of this story are brown bears, also known as grizzly bears in the interior of northwestern North America. From Scandinavia, clear across Siberia, and into North America, they are both the same species, *Ursus arctos*, which means bear in Latin and Greek, respectively. For thousands of years, brown bears have evoked fear in humans and for good reason. They can weigh up to almost one ton (the Kodiak bear, a brown bear of coastal Alaska, grows even larger than a polar bear), run faster than the fastest human, and with a massive paw smash the spine of a moose. And they are very unpredictable. Yet a visitor to a national park in bear country is about three hundred times more likely to be killed by a car than a bear.

But fear is not the sole reason why native peoples have respected bears. Traditionally they have felt kinship with bears, considering them our closest animal relatives. Indeed one traditional name for bears used by the Haida is Elder Kinsman. For the Haida and other Pacific Northwest cultures, bears are a powerful totem and are important family crests. To the Cree in central Canada, bears have been known as Four-Legged Humans. Like humans, bears are intelligent and curious. They often stand on their hind legs, walk upright, and pick berries in the same manner as a person. Like humans, they are omnivores—they can eat almost anything, preferring highly nutritious food they can get easily and in large quantity (therefore, except for coastal brown bears with easy access to salmon, they are 80 to 90 percent vegetarian). It's understandable why many tribes would not eat bear meat, believing it was like eating a person, a relative. The famous naturalist John Muir called bears our "hairy brothers." They could as well be called our hairy sisters, or mothers.

Bears are good mothers. Cubs are not born knowing how to be bears; they must learn from their mothers (the males take no part in rearing cubs). Cubs nurse for one year, and a yearling would have little chance of surviving without its mother. But by age two or three years, the young bear's mother will chase it away; by then, the cub will be ready. It will be big and strong and smart.

Yet in spite of their great strength and intelligence, in the lower forty-eight states, where there are less than eighteen hundred left, brown bears are listed as threatened by the Endangered Species Act. The last grizzly in the "Golden Bear State" of California was shot in 1922. Thousands still roam in Alaska, northwestern Canada, and Russia, but even in these areas brown bears are rapidly disappearing. Can we learn once again to share the land with the bears, as native people once learned? Grizzlies need space. Can't we afford to give space to Honey Paw and Lightfoot? Can we afford not to?

For Jonathan, thanks for writing such paintable words . . . —JVZ

For Barbara Kouts, special agent; with thanks to Grizzly men Doug Peacock and Andy Russell —J. L.

First edition printed by Chronicle Books, 1995

Alaska Northwest Books®
An imprint of

P.O. Box 56118
Portland, OR 97238-6118
(503) 254-5591
www.graphicartsbooks.com

Library of Congress Cataloging in Publication Data

London, Jonathan, 1947–
Honey Paw and Lightfoot by Jonathon London;
illustrated by Jon Van Zyle
p. cm.
Summary: After giving birth in her winter den, Honey Paw, a brown bear cares for her cub and teaches him how to survive in the wild
ISBN: 978-1-941821-10-7
1. Brown bear—Juvenile fiction. [1. Brown bear—Fiction. 2. Bears—Fiction. 3. Animals—Infancy, Fiction.] I. Van Zyle, Jon, ill. II. Title.
PX10-3.l8534Ho 1994
[E]—dc20 94-1030
CIP

4.2.14
Printed by Guangzhou Yi Cai Printing (Guangzhou China), Co. Ltd
J131115FC03